Clifford The BIG RED DOG®

WATCH ON prime video PBS KIDS

The Fire Dog Challenge

Clifford created by
Norman Bridwell

Scholastic Inc.

Written by
Meredith Rusu

Copyright © 2020 by Scholastic Entertainment Inc.
CLIFFORD, CLIFFORD THE BIG RED DOG, and associated logos are trademarks and/or registered trademarks of The Norman Bridwell Trust.

PBS KIDS and PBS KIDS logo are trademarks of Public Broadcasting Service. Used with permission.

All rights reserved. Published by Scholastic Inc., *Publishers since 1920.* SCHOLASTIC and associated logos are trademarks and/or registered trademarks of Scholastic Inc.

The publisher does not have any control over and does not assume any responsibility for author or third-party websites or their content.

No part of this publication may be reproduced, stored in a retrieval system, or transmitted in any form or by any means, electronic, mechanical, photocopying, recording, or otherwise, without written permission of the publisher. For information regarding permission, write to Scholastic Inc., Attention: Permissions Department, 557 Broadway, New York, NY 10012.

This book is a work of fiction. Names, characters, places, and incidents are either the product of the author's imagination or are used fictitiously, and any resemblance to actual persons, living or dead, business establishments, events, or locales is entirely coincidental.

ISBN 978-1-338-66508-6

10 9 8 7 6 5 4 3 2 1   20 21 22 23 24

Printed in Jefferson City, MO, U.S.A. 40 • First edition 2020

Scholastic Inc., 557 Broadway, New York, NY 10012
Scholastic UK Ltd., Euston House, 24 Eversholt Street, London NW1 1DB
Scholastic LTD, Unit 89E, Lagan Road, Dublin Industrial Estate, Glasnevin, Dublin 11

Clifford, Emily Elizabeth, and Tucker were gathered in front of the Birdwell Island firehouse.

Tucker was wearing his special vest and hat. Today was his Fire Dog Challenge!

"If I do well today, Fire Chief Franklin will give me my Bravery Badge!" Tucker told Clifford.

Tucker had already earned his Safety Badge, First Aid Badge, and Patrol Badge. There was just one empty spot left.

"Once I earn my Bravery Badge, I'll be a real fire dog!" he said.

"I know you can do it," Clifford told him. "You've been practicing for the challenge for weeks."

When the challenge started, Fire Chief Franklin explained the rules.

"I'm going to give you three tasks to test your bravery," he told Tucker. "If you do well, you'll earn your Bravery Badge! Are you ready?"

"Rrrufff!" Tucker barked. He was *definitely* ready!

"The first task is about teamwork," Fire Chief Franklin said. "When you hear the fire alarm, pass these fire buckets down the line to us."

Tucker wagged his tail and got into position.

"Ready . . . set . . . go!"

BRRRRRRIIIIIINNNNG!

The fire station alarm blared.

"Yeeeeeep!" Tucker squealed. He'd never practiced with a real alarm before.

The loud noise scared him! He leapt into a pair of fire pants to hide.

"Are you okay?" Emily Elizabeth asked.

But Tucker could barely stop shaking.

"Let's try the second task," suggested the Fire Chief.

He led them outside. "Every good fire dog needs to be quick. I want you to pull the fire hose through this tunnel as fast as you can. Think you can do it, buddy?"

"Ruff!" Tucker was still a little shaky. But he was going to try!

"Go!" said the Fire Chief.

Tucker sprinted through the tunnel. He was doing great!

But suddenly, a creature blocked his path. A sticky, slimy, green creature. It was a frog!

"Eeeeep!" Tucker yelped. He ran right back out to where he'd started.

"What happened?" Clifford asked Tucker.

"I keep getting scared," Tucker said sadly. "Maybe I'm not up to the fire dog challenge after all."

"You just need to focus," Clifford encouraged him.

It was time for the last task.

Fire Chief Franklin was going to pull up in the fire truck.

It was Tucker's job to push the button that closed the fire station door.

But the truck had a loud siren. Would Tucker get scared?

WEEEEE-WOOOOO! WEEEEE-WOOOOO!

"YELP!" went Tucker. He hid inside the firefighter pants again when he heard the siren.

"It's no use," Tucker groaned to Clifford. "What kind of fire dog is afraid of flashing lights and fire alarms?"

"Don't give up," Emily Elizabeth patted Tucker's back. "I know you can do it—I'll prove it!"

She showed him a book about the history of fire dogs.

"It says here that Dalmatians have always been great fire dogs because they're loyal, quick, and bold. Tucker, you're a Dalmatian! You've got everything it takes!"

"Do you think those Dalmatians were ever scared?" Tucker asked Clifford.

"Of course," Clifford said. "Being brave means helping others even when you're scared."

"I never thought of it like that." Tucker wagged his tail.

Just then, the fire station alarm went off again. But this wasn't a test—it was real!

Tucker jumped, but he didn't hide.

"There's an emergency down at Rocky Point!" Fire Chief Franklin came running in. "But the fire truck has a flat tire."

"Oh, no!" cried Emily Elizabeth. "How will you get there?"

"Ruff!" Tucker had an idea. He nudged Emily Elizabeth toward Clifford.

"Tucker's right!" Emily Elizabeth realized. "We may not have a big red fire truck. But we *do* have a big red dog!"

Together, the friends hopped up on Clifford and raced to Rocky Point.

Mrs. Clayton was there when they arrived.

"My little kitty, Willa, fell into a deep crack in the rocks, and now she can't get out!" Mrs. Clayton cried.

"Oh, no! We've got to help her!" said Emily Elizabeth.

But Fire Chief Franklin frowned. "The hole is too small for any of us to fit inside."

"Ruff, ruff!" Tucker hopped into the fire pail and wagged his tail. *He* was small enough to fit in the hole.

"Good thinking, Tucker!" said Fire Chief Franklin. "We can lower you down in the bucket. But it will be dark. Are you sure?"

"Woof!" Tucker nodded. He had to be brave!

Carefully, the friends lowered Tucker into the hole. He gulped. It *was* very dark.

"But Willa must be even more scared," he thought. "I have to help her."

Mustering his courage, Tucker reached out and pulled Willa up into the pail.

"You're safe now," he said.

"You rescued Willa!" Mrs. Clayton cried when they pulled the bucket back up. "Thank you, Tucker. You were so brave."

"You really were," agreed the Fire Chief. "That's why you've earned your Bravery Badge!"

"Ruff?" Tucker barked in surprise.

"You were speedy, quick-thinking, and worked with your team when it mattered," Fire Chief Franklin explained. "Any dog who can do that is brave enough to be a fire dog."

Tucker jumped and wagged his tail.

"Hooray for Tucker!" cheered his friends. "The newest Birdwell Island Fire Dog!"

FIRE DOG TUCKER'S FIRE SAFETY TIPS

Being brave starts with staying safe. Follow these fire safety tips every day:

1) Don't play with matches or lighters. And never, ever use them without an adult's help.

2) Stay away from open flames or sources of heat, like stoves or fireplaces.

3) Talk with your parents about what to do in an emergency. Practice an escape plan so you always know how to get to safety.

4) If you are in a fire, stay low and get out! Wait to call 911 until you are somewhere safe.

5) If your clothes ever catch fire, stop, drop, and roll to snuff out the flame.

6) Remind your parents to change the batteries in all the smoke detectors in your home twice a year.

USA • PO# 5020087 • 06/20